Dear Mr. President

Dear Mr. President

Thomas Jefferson
Letters from a Philadelphia Bookworm

by Jennifer Armstrong

WINSLOW PRESS

Florida • New York

A Note From the Publisher

In our *Dear Mr. President* series, the text is in the form of
letters exchanged between President Thomas Jefferson and a
twelve-year-old girl, Amelia Hornsby. Although the letters
are fictional, the information in them is based on meticulous
research. In an effort to capture President Jefferson's personality,
and the youth of that time, as well as facts about Lewis and
Clark's famous expedition, the author relied on such books as
Lewis and Clark: Pioneering Naturalists by Paul Russell Cutright,
The Garden and Farm Books of Thomas Jefferson, *In Pursuit of
Reason: The Life of Thomas Jefferson* by Noble Cunningham,
and *If You Were There When They Signed the Constitution* by
Elizabeth Levy.

Information on the city of Philadelphia in 1780 was gained
from source material such as *Philadelphia: A 300 Year History*,
edited by Russell F. Weigley. A list of recommended reading
can be found on pages 102–105.

It is our hope that the *Dear Mr. President* books and their
portrayal of issues from other eras will provide readers with
valuable insights into important moments in American
history. Each title, written by a skilled author, is further
enhanced by interactive footnotes, games, activities, and
links, with detailed historical information at the book's own
Web site in our virtual library, winslowpress.com.

By offering you a rich reading experience coupled with
our interactive Web site, we encourage you to embrace the
future with what is best from the past.

Diane F. Kessenich, Publisher and CEO, Winslow Press

"Lewis and Clark's Trail," reproduced by Robert Vaughn, 1905

Dear Mr. President,

Sincerely,

Amelia Hornsby

Dear Miss Amelia Hornsby,

Sincerely,

Th. Jefferson

Introduction

At the beginning of the 1800s, America was still a brand-new country. Its citizens were still learning who they were and where they might go in their new surroundings. To lead them, they had one of the most talented and brilliant presidents this country has ever seen: Thomas Jefferson. He was not only a statesman and politician. He was not only the man who drafted our revolutionary Declaration of Independence. He was also a musician, a scientist, an inventor, an engineer, an architect, a gardener, a family man, a friend, and a philosopher. Perhaps no other president in American history has come close to his incredible range of interests, skills, and talents.

In addition to being the third president of the United States, Thomas Jefferson was the president of the American Philosophical Society in Philadelphia. Philadelphia was the largest, most intellectual, and most sophisticated city in America at that time. The American Philosophical Society included some of the country's most respected scientists and thinkers.

Imagine, then, a girl named Amelia Hornsby living during the early 1800s in Philadelphia. In this city, she would have rubbed elbows with some of the brightest lights in the country. She would have received a good education in Philadelphia, which had very progressive ideas about schooling. And she would have taken an active and lively interest in the current events and political affairs of her day, even writing to the president if she felt it was her duty. Imagine Amelia writing to President Jefferson.

The port of Philadelphia, 1800

To learn more about the Declaration of Independence, visit winslowpress.com.

Independence Hall, Philadelphia, 1900

Philadelphia
To Mr. Thomas Jefferson at The President's House
Washington City

Dear Sir,

I may have bad manners to annoy you with such a letter. But my concern for the importance of your office begs me to speak. I give no thought to possible embarrassment, although it may be lurking like a snake in the grass. However, I cannot let such worries shut my mouth or stay my pen. To do so would be cowardly.

My guardian is known to you. He is the good Dr. Benjamin Rush of this city. Yesterday when I returned from school, I found a man awaiting Dr. Rush in the drawing room. He claimed his name as Meriwether Lewis and said that he was on a secret commission from you, the president. He went on with another astonishing statement: that he is your personal secretary. He is a very bold young man and hardly seems fit to hold such an important position. When I demanded proofs of his claim, he bade me seek them out from you.

I cannot tell if he was teasing me. But I am not one of the sort that takes well to teasing. Therefore, sir, I wish to inform you that either a young scoundrel is making false claims in your name, or your secretary is overfond of teasing.

Dutifully your servant,

Amelia Hornsby

Amelia Hornsby, Patriot

Engraving of Meriwether Lewis by Charles Balthazar Julien Feret de Saint–Mémin, 1805

To learn more about Meriwether Lewis, visit winslowpress.com.

April 25, 1803

Washington City
To Miss Amelia Hornsby
Philadelphia

Dear Miss Amelia Hornsby,

I thank you for your patriotic warning and pray you rest easy on this score. No doubt you have learned full well by now through assurances from Dr. Rush that indeed Mr. Meriwether Lewis is my personal secretary. I have sent him to Philadelphia on an especial charge. He is to fill the gaps in his knowledge of certain topics: medical, botanical, meteorological, et cetera. And these gaps are to be filled by the most highly esteemed Dr. Rush and by diverse other learned gentlemen of the American Philosophical Society there in Philadelphia.

Truly, it has often seemed a serious drawback that the capital seat of government was removed from Philadelphia, which was so well endowed with men of learning. Even now, nearly three years since the government was installed here in Washington City, the capital is woefully muddy, unbuilt, and under inhabited by men of distinction, and wanting in polite society. I had no resources suitable to the purpose here as I could find among my old colleagues in Philadelphia. Therefore, it was quite necessary and unavoidable for me to send Lewis there.

Your humble servant,

Thos. Jefferson

Independence Hall, Philadelphia, 1876

May 15, 1803

Philadelphia

Dear Sir,

Mr. Lewis is here often, and I have begged his pardon many times for suspecting him as a spy in the service of a foreign power (for truly, that is what I feared at the start). He is always friendly and familiar, but declines to tell me the nature of his secret plan. Yesterday he dined here in company with Dr. Rush, and recited how Dr. Benjamin Smith Barton has been instructing him in the proper manner for collecting and preserving plant specimens. Further, he explained to me very intelligently the principles of navigation by the stars, as taught to him by Mr. Andrew Ellicott. Yet he continued to evade my questions on the specific nature of his mission.

I believe I have now discovered it. You are preparing him for an expedition into unknown lands—*terra incognita*. I have always been adept at proofs of logic. At Mr. Poor's Academy for Young Ladies I have always enjoyed the mathematical and philosophical sciences the most. My father, who has gone on to Pittsburgh to teach at the new college there (leaving me here in Dr. Rush's care), instructed me from when I was the tiniest child to order my thoughts and think with clarity and reason.

After examining the evidence I have gained from Mr. Lewis, I conclude that you are sending him on a mission into the continent of Africa. Mr. Lewis, to whom I have offered my conclusion, says I must seek the answer from you.

Your servant,

Amelia Hornsby

Amelia Hornsby, Logician

The President's House

Dear Miss Hornsby,

Your grasp of philosophy and logic appears altogether sound. No doubt owing to the example of your father and the example of the good Dr. Rush, you have demonstrated the finest qualities of reason and logic. Mr. Poor must consider himself a fortunate man to have such a fine pupil as yourself.

Forgive me, however, if I beg to put off my answer to your question. Negotiations of the most sensitive nature are yet underway. I must not offer a hasty report. When we may be less guarded and secretive, you will know all. But I can say that your logic is sound, although you err in one important particular.

Meanwhile, convey my best regards to Dr. Rush and Mrs. Rush. I am sure they are delighted with your company, and must be pleased to take you with them into society.

Your servant,

Thos. Jefferson

June 10, 1803

Philadelphia
To Mr. Thomas Jefferson, President
Washington City

Dear Sir,

   I most humbly beg your pardon. I am not yet in society, having passed through a mere twelve years on this earth. This is why I reside with Dr. Rush while waiting for my father to establish a home for me on the frontier at Pittsburgh. My mother was taken in the yellow fever epidemic in 1798, as were my sisters and brothers. I alone survive with my father.

From poor

Amelia Hornsby

Amelia Hornsby, Half-orphan

Dr. Benjamin Rush during the time he taught medicine at the University of Pennsylvania

The President's House

My Dear Miss Amelia,

   The maturity of your sentiments must have led me astray. I confess I did assume you to be a young woman already in society, and an uncommonly well-educated one, at that. I think I may say that Dr. Rush and Mrs. Rush must be all the more pleased with your company. Indeed, upon Mr. Lewis's return here last week, he agreed that you are a most sensible and intelligent young person, and that you ask a rather extraordinary number of questions.

   Tomorrow Mr. Lewis begins his journey. Now, as the news becomes official tomorrow, I can say that you were right in your hazard of Lewis's mission—up to your guess of destination, at any event. The Corps of Discovery, as we call it, is to seek out a navigable route through the rivers of our own continent. They must do so by traveling up the Mississippi River and from there, up through the waters of the Missouri River. Our

sensitive negotiations with France have resulted in our purchase of the entire Louisiana Territory—not just of the city of New Orleans, which we had wished at the start. France is entangled in its own political events at home, and does not wish to be burdened by a vast, unexplored section of North America. I own I often dreamed of such an outcome, but hardly dared give voice to my secret hopes.

Map of the Louisiana Territory drawn from surveys, assisted by the most approved English and French maps and charts, the whole being regulated by astronomical observations, by Emanuel Bowen

To learn more about the Louisiana Purchase, visit winslowpress.com.

We have not yet heard confirmation of these negotiations, but have every confidence they will shortly arrive.

Now the United States will hold sway over a vast land. It is filled with plants and animals as yet unknown to science. It is peopled with the uncouth Indian nations which we pray we may bring into the family of civilized society. Lewis's solemn task is to take greetings from me to those people, and to discover what he can of the interior of this continent, while making a serviceable map for the use and comfort of future travelers. It was for this reason that I sent him to Philadelphia to enlarge his knowledge of plants, animals, weather science, navigation, and other useful arts. The object of his mission is to explore the Missouri River, and such principal streams of it, as, by its course and communication with the waters of the Pacific Ocean, may offer the most direct and practicable water communication across this continent, for the purposes of commerce.

Lewis leaves here in two days for the frontier, where he will meet with William Clark, the second commander of the Corps of Discovery. Their journey will officially begin in the spring, from Saint Louis.

I can think of no finer goal than the exploration of this bountiful North America.

Your servant,

Thos. Jefferson

Thos. Jefferson

To learn more about expressions used in the 1800s, such as "hazard of Lewis's mission," visit winslowpress.com.

To learn more about the Corps of Discovery, visit winslowpress.com.

Philadelphia

Dear Sir,

The great news was published here on July 4, and I do think it a most marvelous undertaking. As I have had the chance to take Mr. Lewis's measure in person, and judge for myself what quality of man he is, I believe you have chosen very well. He is honest, forthright, sensible, curious, brave, courteous, and good. My study of the ancient Greeks and Romans assures me that these are the very best qualities to have in a leader. The members of the Corps of Discovery will follow him willingly.

Also, I think it very fine and generous that part of your aim in sending Mr. Lewis into the wilderness is to bring aid to the poor Indians. Some of the Indian children should be sent here to our cities to be brought up as Christians and taught such arts as may prove useful to them. My father writes in his letter that he often sees Indian children at Fort Pittsburgh, and they are often dirty and ignorant.

This summer it is very hot here in Philadelphia, and Mr. Poor's is closed until such time as the weather improves. I don't believe I've been down Cherry Street past the academy in two weeks. We do have a rare treat when we go to the New Caveau Hotel for iced cream. Such a delicacy! And we also enjoy picnics by the Schuylkill as an escape.

Now, when the heat becomes very bad, I think about Mr. Lewis beginning his great voyage up the Mississippi and Missouri Rivers. The thought of so much water is refreshing!

Respectfully yours,

Amelia Hornsby

Amelia Hornsby, Slow-cooked

To learn more about relations between First Americans and the pioneers, visit winslowpress.com.

Map showing the Mississippi and Missouri Rivers

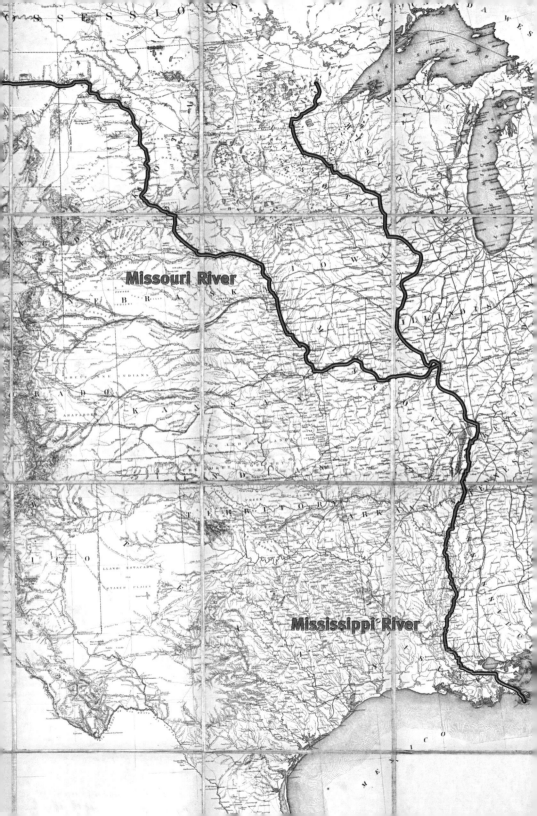

Monticello

Dear Miss Amelia,

I am at my own delightful home, now, and away from the heat of the capital. Philadelphia can certainly be hot in the summer, although by reference to the daily record I keep of the weather, i.e. rainfall, temperature, and wind direction, I know that on that momentous day in 1776 when we signed the Declaration of Independence, Philadelphia was a quite temperate 76 degrees of Mercury at one o'clock in the afternoon. That was unusual, however, as by your own experience you know that Philadelphia is ordinarily quite close and hot in the summer. If you can credit it, however, Washington seems to be even worse, as it is so swampy. The damp heat oppresses the entire city. A sad sight indeed is the number of carriage horses dropping in their tracks. I feel such pity for the poor beasts.

Here on our mountaintop we are charmed with cool breezes, and I find it much easier to get on with my work. My unvaried routine in the mornings is this: I rise the soonest there is enough daylight to read the clock at the foot of my bed, and I then spend three or four hours writing and reading letters. Even now as I write this to you it is not yet half past seven in the morning. Sitting upon my desk is my mockingbird, who is as clever as a Philadelphia lawyer. When I was ambassador to France, I often had the opportunity to hear a true European nightingale sing; and I promise you, our native mockingbird sings as sweetly and much longer through the year. This bird often perches on my shoulder and watches me write, just as if a genie or familiar spirit kept council with me.

After my morning letters are finished, I meet with any cabinet member who comes from the capital to consult with me. I try always to ride for exercise after the noon hour,

---

An etching of Monticello

To learn more about Monticello, visit winslowpress.com.

taking the opportunity to survey the construction projects underway here at Monticello; and then dine at three thirty. My time lately has been so preoccupied with plans for Lewis and Clark's expedition that I am sadly behind in other work. Therefore I continue with my reading and correspondence until I retire, well past the hour of candle-lighting.

Like you, I turn my thoughts often to the men of the Corps of Discovery. When I am fatigued, the thought of their labors to come gives me renewed energy. News from them will be little and much delayed, but I can hardly wait to hear what they find in the interior. Lewis's plan calls for him to depart at the end of this month for Kentucky with such men as he has recruited for the expedition.

I have asked him to observe climate as characterized by the thermometer, by the proportion of rainy, cloudy, and clear days, by lightning, hail, snow, ice; by the access and recess of frost, by the winds prevailing at different seasons, the dates at which particular plants put forth or lose their flowers, or leaf, times of appearance of particular birds, reptiles or insects. As I make my own daily observations in my farm book and garden book, my thoughts stray ever toward Lewis and his company, and toward those remarkable things which he is even now encountering.

With best wishes,

Thos. Jefferson

Philadelphia

Dear Sir,

If it is not too late to send for Mr. Lewis and Mr. Clark, I think I have hit upon a vehicle that could be most advantageous to them in their discoveries. Only yesterday in the afternoon, I was privileged to make an ascension in the *Vertical Aerial Coach*. Mrs. Rush feared that the height would make me giddy, but I am not so light-headed as that. This balloon, by means of gases lighter than our own atmosphere, arose from its tethering spot beside the Schuylkill. When we had ascended to the extent of the tether, I own I could see clear to New Jersey. Below me was the entire city of Philadelphia, along with the docks on the Delaware River. I was even able to spy many familiar city landmarks, including the Chestnut Theatre and Mr. Asbury Dickins's Bookshop opposite Christ Church, from this position. The descent was every bit as interesting as the ascent was, in spite of my stomach not wishing to return to Earth at quite the same rate. I am quite determined now to become an aerialist.

You must see if it be not possible for Mr. Lewis and Mr. Clark to take with them on their heroic expedition one of these balloons. Nothing will serve their purpose half so well. With the aid of such a balloon they will be able to discover all the lands 'round about them, and when navigation becomes uncertain it will assist them in choosing the right course.

Respectfully yours,

Amelia Hornsby

Amelia Hornsby, Aeronaut

A drawing of a traveling balloon (A) with a circumference of 2,000 feet. Note the cabin (C), rudder (B), and spiral fan wheel (D). It is similar to the Vertical Aerial Coach *described by Amelia Hornsby, although it was designed at a later date and appeared in* Mechanics *Magazine in 1834.*

September 12, 1803

Washington City
To Miss Amelia Hornsby
Philadelphia

Dear Miss Amelia,

I do indeed thank you for your very good suggestion about the balloon. I fear, however, that the Corps of Discovery has no way to produce the gas needed to fill the bag. They are traveling into unsettled territory, and must carry all their equipment and supplies with them. Such things as they will carry include rifle powder, flints, portable soup, salt, mosquito netting, ink powder, and assorted trinkets and goods for trade with the Indians.

The vehicle best suited to their purposes is a keelboat, which was constructed for them in Pittsburgh to Lewis's specifications. This said boat was designed to be fifty-five feet long, eight feet wide, having a shallow draught. It should carry a mast and square sail, and be able to carry a burden of twelve tons. Their route lies on the water. I applaud your advice that a balloon would provide a distant survey. However, as it is equally important that the flora and fauna along the way be investigated, travel on the ground level is the best choice.

I will confess to you that the investigation of flora and fauna is almost my chief concern. I believe that among the greatest goods a man can do is to introduce a useful and practical plant to civilization. I look forward to the day in the future when I can plant some new discovery in my gardens at Monticello. Further, I wish to allay certain prejudices held by the scientists of Europe, who claim that the animals of North America are puny and degenerate by comparison to the animals of Europe. Our native moose-deer has proved them wrong already; but I am convinced that even greater and more magnificent animals are yet to be found in the interior.

I have in my natural history cabinet a great curiosity, to wit, the fossil bone of an unknown, massive creature, which was discovered in Greenbrier County, Virginia. I gave this creature the name *Megalonyx*, as I am persuaded it was a massive, lionlike beast; if you have enough Latin, you will know that megalonyx means "Great Claw"; and the name should give you some indication of the fearsomeness of the talons. If such animals yet live on this continent, such discovery should put an end to the debate once and for all. And lest you counter that a hot-air balloon would give the best vantage point for espying giant animals, it is also true that walking on the riverbanks gives the best vantage for discovering the fossils that lie within the soil.

Your servant,

Thos. Jefferson

To learn more about archaeology in the 19th century, visit winslowpress.com.

Etching of a moose

31

September 29, 1803

Philadelphia
To Mr. Thomas Jefferson, President
Washington City

Dear Sir,

Now you have touched upon another one of my especial passions. I, too, have a natural history cabinet. You will not be surprised to learn that this passion was inspired by my first visit to Mr. Peale's Repository for Natural Curiosities. I first saw these wonders shortly after the collection was removed to Philosophical Hall. I was a mere toddling child at the time, yet they aroused in me such interest in the natural world. I began at once to dig for bones and fossils in the kitchen garden. Alas, I succeeded only in dismaying my dear mother, who had but that day planted her carrot seeds.

Since those infant attempts I have added many interesting specimens to my cabinet. I have a stone which I am quite certain is an arrowhead of Indian manufacture. I own it is possible that the shape is due to natural causes. But it looks uncommonly like an arrowhead.

If indeed the Corps of Discovery should find fossils of a new animal, or indeed the animal itself, this will be cause for jubilation.

If it is not an impertinence, I should like to make one additional suggestion for something the Corps of Discovery might find useful. We hear that Mr. Fulton has been experimenting with a steam-driven underwater boat or submarine which he calls *Nautilus*. There is a mollusk or shellfish of that name, I understand. He is at present making these experiments in the Seine River in Paris, but perhaps we may expect him to return to his native land. He is, you know, from Pennsylvania. If this submarine boat is indeed capable of navigating rivers, perhaps Mr. Lewis and Mr. Clark could make use of it? I am not quite sure if this boat has windows or portholes. But if so, it would provide an excellent view of the fishes of the American rivers and any other curiosities that lie beneath the waters.

School has resumed at Mr. Poor's. I am asked to give a speech on a topic of my choosing. I am not sure if I should declaim on the Entry of Ohio into the Union, or What We May Expect from the Invention of the Steam-powered Loom Should It Be Introduced into General Industrial Practice.

Respectfully yours,

Amelia Hornsby

Amelia Hornsby, Orator

(Left) Detail of etching of Robert Fulton. (Right) Print of Nautilus

To learn more about Robert Fulton, visit winslowpress.com.

To learn more about Charles Willson Peale and his Repository for Natural Curiosities, visit winslowpress.com.

Washington City

Dear Miss Amelia,

Once again, your advice is much appreciated. Sadly, the technology of this submarine vessel is yet in its infancy. The rigors of the expedition are such that only a vehicle powered by strength of arms and the currents of water is possible. Fuel to power such a steam-driven submarine boat would be too toilsome to gather and carry. But as I say, your advice is very gratefully received. I only regret we cannot use it.

If you have not yet made your oration, I might relate some interesting facts that could be used to illustrate a lecture on Ohio. I have heard from Mr. Lewis, who is descending the Ohio River from Pittsburgh. He reports that on September 13, passenger pigeons were seen migrating south in such vast multitudes that they obscured the sun. In addition, he reported seeing squirrels migrating across the Ohio River from north to south. Lewis has acquired a dog which he calls Seaman, and this said dog leaped from the keelboat after the swimming squirrels, retrieving one after another until enough were had for dinner. The squirrels were eaten fried. This may perhaps be of interest if you decide to prepare an oration on Ohio.

By now I hope that Lewis has reached the Indiana Territory, where he will finally meet up with William Clark. My eagerness chafes at the long delays I must expect before hearing news from the party.

Respectfully yours,

Thos. Jefferson

To learn more about William Clark, visit winslowpress.com.

Seaman was said to be a big dog like this one.

Portrait of William Clark by Charles Willson Peale Background: Map of western territory made by fur traders, 1807

November 17, 1803

Philadelphia
To Mr. Thomas Jefferson, President
Washington City

Dear Sir,

You may wonder at not hearing from me for some weeks. Allow me to explain.

As perhaps you know, Philadelphia put a water works into operation at the outset of 1801. Since that time, more and more houses and manufactories have been joined to this water system. As a consequence of this, many streets are being dug to lay pipes and install hydrants, where the public may draw water conveniently. On the day I received your last letter to me (and may I say it was very interesting what you said about the pigeons and squirrels), I was studying the laying out of some of these water pipes. I had paused on my way from school, and was about to explain some of the principles of hydrodynamics (being of course the movement of water) to the working men who labored in the ditch. I have been fortunate to be given an education. Therefore I think it only seemly to instruct those less fortunate than I, when given the chance. Do you not think it our duty to enlighten the ignorant? So I was preparing to instruct these men, only I was a little shy because they were so rough-looking; and I was unable to attract their notice while they bantered with one another. So I hesitated on the brink, as it were, and the shout of a street vender yelling "Pepper pot, nice and hot!" just behind me gave me such a start that I toppled into the trench. It would have been very interesting to me to examine

To learn more about Philadelphia's water works, visit winslowpress.com.

these workings from this closer position, but I became sensible of a sharp pain in one of my limbs. This prevented me from discussing water pressure with the laborers, who anyway were busy hauling me out and running for a doctor. And I fear there was some cursing, as well, although it shames me to admit I heard it.

My esteemed guardian diagnosed a broken ankle. The pain has been very severe and has made me too gloomy for writing letters. But I hope I am not so puny that I would mope forever. I will soon be allowed to hobble about with a cane, and will return to my studies as soon as I am able.

Respectfully yours,

Amelia Hornsby

Amelia Hornsby, Invalid

Washington City

Dear Miss Amelia,

   May God speed your recovery. You are in good hands with my old friend Dr. Rush for a physician. I fear your natural curiosity is perhaps a risky one. Learn to temper your avid nature with prudence. Consider how doomed to failure the Corps of Discovery would be had they not a prudent man leading them. I trust Mr. Lewis is as curious an explorer as I could wish to find; but he is cautious, withal. I could not entrust such a momentous journey to a man who did not know how to be careful.

   The Corps of Discovery left in late November for Saint Louis; and I hope they have lately come there. That city is settled in the main by Canadians of French origin, and is the center of the fur trade. The men are to winter in the vicinity of Saint Louis, making their final preparations for the voyage up the Mississippi to the Missouri. Also, in Saint Louis, the official transfer of Louisiana Territory from France to the United States will take place. After that, the men will begin their exploration of American territory. I trust you will join with me in praying that this New Year will see their journey safely under way.

Your servant,

Thos. Jefferson

P.S. Jan. 22—I have kept this letter open till today, as I was expecting a letter from Dr. Rush himself; and as it has arrived, and he has given a good account of your recovery, I am content to send this off now with further wishes for your safe return to school.

To learn more about
the fur trade, visit
winslowpress.com.

*Photogravure of painting by J.W. Duel of the transfer of
Upper Louisiana Territory to the United States at St.
Louis, March, 1804*

February 11, 1804

Philadelphia
To Mr. Thomas Jefferson, President
Washington City

Dear Sir,

You may trust that I have tried mightily to learn prudence. I know it is a virtue and one I should acquire. I think I may say I am prudent at intervals. However, the intervals do not always line up properly with circumstances. Only the day before my accident I was very prudent and cautious when I was asked to recite the 102nd Psalm and was not exactly sure of my wording. Rather than give offense by misquoting the Psalm, I replied that just then a runaway horse was charging past the schoolroom window. Before the uproar caused by this announcement died away, I had had the opportunity to review the text.

Now, I admit that this was a falsehood, and falsehoods are vile. But is not misquoting the Psalm equally bad? And yet, now that I consider it, perhaps I had another way open to me, and that was to admit I did not know how to recite the Psalm. My father has often rebuked me for pride and vanity; but because I am not a fussy, maidenish sort of girl taken by fashion, I thought he was unfair. Now I think perhaps he detects pride and vanity of a different sort in me: is it wrong to be so fond of knowledge?

Respectfully yours,

Amelia Hornsby

Amelia Hornsby, Penitent

Juniper and High Streets, Philadelphia, early 1800s

March 1, 1804

Washington
To Miss Amelia Hornsby
Philadelphia

Dear Miss Amelia,

Do not punish yourself overmuch. You have detected a fault in yourself. Rather than heap abuse on your own head, strive to overcome this fault. There is no shame in seeking knowledge, and no shame in loving knowledge. It has always been the polestar of my own life. But try to be humble in your pursuit of knowledge. Never fear to admit your ignorance. It is only by asking questions that we learn.

Your servant,

Thos. Jefferson

Early water buckets for putting out fires

To learn more about fire-fighting in the 19th century, visit winslowpress.com.

Philadelphia

Dear Sir,

You might remark on the long interval since your letter to me. I have been engaged in a very interesting project betimes. One month ago, there was a stable fire in Whale Bone Alley here in the city, and it was extinguished by the power of a fire hose carriage from North Fourth Street. This was a noteworthy demonstration of how useful this invention is. There was some concern that the crowd which had gathered to watch the operation of the hose carriage might obstruct the men who fought the flames so valiantly. It was as curious a sight as a two-headed baby. I myself might have been slightly in the way for a few moments, but as the fire did not spread, I am sure I did no harm.

The upshot of this remarkable event was that subscriptions were taken up to form two more hose companies for the city. May I with some small modesty inform you that I led the vanguard among the young ladies at Mr. Poor's? I exhorted them daily for two weeks to give up their pin money. I am very satisfied to say that I carried the day. The collection plate held such a combination of French Louis and Portuguese gold coins and Spanish milled dollars and old shillings and new pence that it was difficult to know quite how much it really added up to. But we presented the sum to the editor of the Port Folio, who was heading the subscription.

I was ever so proud to see my own name listed in the Port Folio the following week among the list of other subscribers.

Respectfully yours,

Amelia Hornsby

Amelia Hornsby, Philanthropist

April 20, 1804

Philadelphia
To Mr. Thomas Jefferson, President
Washington City

Dear Sir,

My deepest condolences on the death of your dear daughter Maria. Dr. Rush brought the news to us last night when he joined us for family dinner. What a dreadful thing to lose your daughter and grandbaby! My heart aches in sympathy for you. It recalls to me when I lost my dear mother, and I am shrouded with grief.

Perhaps you do not wish to be pestered with the foolish chatter of a girl, and so I will refrain from sending more letters to you.

Respectfully yours,

Amelia Hornsby

Amelia Hornsby

To learn more about Jefferson's family, visit winslowpress.com.

Detail of portrait of Thomas Jefferson

June 25, 1804

Monticello
To Miss Amelia Hornsby
Philadelphia

Dear Miss Amelia,

It has been a very long time since I wrote to you. By means of a polygraph machine made for me by Mr. Peale, I am able to make copies of every letter I write as I write it; and so I see that I last wrote to you in early March. It pains me to see that I never replied to your very kind letter of condolence to me, nor did I hasten to reassure you that your letters are not a bother to me. On the contrary, it is water to a thirsty man to have letters that do not beg or cajole, wheedle, bargain, or complain. That is the nature of so many of my letters that I grow very weary of the business of politics. I almost hesitate to open my correspondence some days, for fear of finding a furious insult in bold ink. So I assure you, my dear young friend, that your letters are a pleasure and I open them with alacrity.

Happily, I am taking a holiday from the dreary business of being president. Here I am in my own dear home. Today our wheat harvest is begun. At the start of the season I feared we should be late, for the spring was very cold and windy here. My daughter Martha, who lives here with her children as hostess at Monticello, reported that they had fires every day during the whole month of April, a very unusual necessity. But as it happened, the weather improved and managed to match itself to the calendar.

It is my settled habit to record the temperature every day, and make a general note of the weather conditions. As a farmer, I find this information exceptionally useful, as it allows me to compare growing conditions from one year to another. I am sure that Dr. Rush has in his possession a meteorological thermometer and barometer. If so, I advise you to acquire the habit of recording the weather in a diary-book or daily log.

Upon reflection, however, I imagine it might be more depressing than interesting to record exactly how hot it is in Philadelphia right now. Perhaps you might wish to begin your meteorological observations in the cooler months of autumn!

Respectfully yours,

Thos. Jefferson

Etching of Martha Jefferson Randolph. Background: Front of Monticello, photo by Theodore Horydczak

To see an excerpt from Jefferson's weather journals, visit winslowpress.com.

July 19, 1804

Philadelphia
To Mr. Thos. Jefferson, President
Washington City

Dear Sir,

The bloodthirsty duello between Vice President Burr and Mr. Hamilton has all the gossips of Philadelphia in an uproar. I am sure you have been much engaged in discussions on the subject, and I have no wish to irritate your patience with more. But certainly Hamilton was a rival to you in politics, and although it would be a sin to be glad of his death, perhaps you are not sorry he is no longer a plague and a pestilence for you to battle. What Mr. Burr's fate will be is the subject of much debate here.

But I am particularly curious to hear of your visit from the chieftain of the Osage Indians, and to hear what news you have of the Corps of Discovery. After their winter in Saint Louis, they must have embarked on their journey some months now. I pray you, what intelligence do you have of them and what reports did they make?

I might add that I am particularly curious for news of the frontier. I will tell you why. My father has written to me that he has at last furnished a suitable home for us. I am to join my father at Pittsburgh as soon as the summer's heat has lifted. So I am soon to be on the frontier, myself.

Respectfully yours,

Amelia Hornsby

Amelia Hornsby, Pioneer

Etching of duel between Aaron Burr (with pistol on left) and Alexander Hamilton (with pistol on right), in which Hamilton was killed.

To learn more about the duel between Aaron Burr and Alexander Hamilton, visit winslowpress.com.

Washington City
To Miss Amelia Hornsby at Dr. Rush's in Philadelphia

Dear Miss Amelia,

I hope this letter will find its way to you, if you have quit Philadelphia already. I am sure you feel a great joy at your reunion with your father, although tempered with sadness at leaving your friends and benefactors, the Rushes. I pray that Pittsburgh will have many interesting and noteworthy attractions for you. No city can compare with Philadelphia, alas, least of all one so new as Pittsburgh. But a person of your curiosity and temperament will no doubt find much matter for occupation.

You asked after the Corps of Discovery, and what news I may have had that might be useful to you in your new home. Before their departure in May, Lewis and Clark had the good fortune to hire two half-breed French Indians, Pierre Cruzatte and Francis Labiche. Both are skilled in the sign languages of the Plains Indians, and in diverse Indian languages such as Omaha, and will be of great service to the Corps. If I can give you any advice for the frontier it is this: seek out every opportunity to learn new languages. My captains are adept at many things, but without the power to communicate with the native tribes they will meet on their journey, they would be much hindered. Lewis highly esteems Labiche and Cruzatte and swore them in as privates of the company.

Beyond this the report was largely of their winter preparations. I chafe at the inevitable delay before I get more news.

Respectfully yours,

Th. Jefferson

**To learn more about
the Lewis and Clark expedition,
visit winslowpress.com.**

Pittsburgh

Dear Sir,

Your letter was much delayed in reaching me. Dr. Rush attempted to forward it to me, but the commercial traveler to whom he entrusted that charge took ill on the road and was forced to return to Philadelphia. That man neglected to return your letter to Dr. Rush for some time. Then my former guardian entrusted it to an itinerant silhouette cutter who had claimed to be moving to Pittsburgh. But that man, too, was not as good as his word. Your letter languished some further time until it was directed to Philadelphia again. At last, Dr. Rush was able to discharge his duty by giving the letter to a Mr. Dickerson, who was moving here to Pittsburgh to open a mercantile.

I find Pittsburgh not nearly as wild as I had feared. We have a large circle of educated acquaintances, all families connected with the new college where my father teaches. Many of the young people of my age are sadly backward, owing to their being brought up so far from the artistic center of the country—that fair city where I so lately dwelled. I have sought friendships among the girls from these families, although they are all younger than I am. They do tend to view me as a miracle of learning and civilization, and do often beg me to "tell them everything."

I am encouraging them to keep a daily record of the weather, as I now do myself. Today we have 33 degrees of Mercury.

Respectfully yours,

Amelia Hornsby

Amelia Hornsby, Oracle

P.S. I am very glad to know you were re-elected for another term as president, and if its your best judgment that Aaron Burr should no longer serve as vice president, I am sure that is quite correct.

Monticello

To Miss Amelia Hornsby at Pittsburgh

Dear Miss Amelia,

Warmest Christmas blessings to you and your father. We are making a celebration of the season here at our dear home. My grandchildren are all about me and having great fun "ice-skating" on our new French floor. This is a technique called parquet which I observed during my years in France. Strips of diverse-colored woods are inlayed in a regular pattern, making an effect much like a chessboard. The wood is cherry of a deep mahogany color, and a very pale beechwood. My grandchildren find it quite an original, and are polishing it by gliding across it in their stocking feet. Here on the eve of Christmas we are experiencing some looseness of manners! I find myself wishing to spend as much time as possible here with my family. The cares and worries of being president weigh heavily upon me; and I cannot help but believe public employment contributes neither to advantage nor happiness. It is but honorable exile from one's family and affairs. However, there is much work to do that I must not shirk.

As I contemplated the fun my grandchildren were having with the French floor, it entered my imagination to wonder how my explorers are spending this Christmas in the wilderness, far, far from such civilized comforts. I hope that you are finding that Pittsburgh is less frontier town and more civilized city as each month passes by.

Respectfully yours,

Th. Jefferson

Pittsburgh

Dear Sir,

You will wonder at the lateness of my reply to your very kind letter at Christmastime. We have had great excitement here and I regret I have been very slow in answering my letters.

In the second week of this New Year we were very happy to receive my second cousin, Josiah Hornsby of the Baltimore Hornsbys. He is to attend the college here at Pittsburgh and share our home with us. It was always his greatest wish to study under the guidance of my father, and so he has come here to the rough-and-tumble frontier! He finds it very different from Baltimore.

He came by way of Philadelphia, bringing all manner of news from that city and from our dear friends there. The new Permanent Bridge at Market Street over the Schuylkill was opened on January 1, and he reports that a cover is planned. How I wish I could have been there to see the opening ceremony! All previous bridges washed away in spring floods, but this bridge is expected to last the ages, and that is why it was christened with such a hopeful name. Cousin Hornsby was good enough to bring several issues of the *Port Folio*, the *Philadelphia Repository*, and the *Weekly Register* with him. I fell upon them as a starving man falls upon a plate of food! I have missed many wonderful things since I left that city. There have been several traveling shows I would have liked to have seen: African animals, a ventriloquist, a phrenologist, Italian paintings, and a practitioner of legerdemain. Cousin Hornsby also brought to me a book on the art of legerdemain, the "sleight of hand." I have been much occupied trying to learn the techniques described in this book. I think it cannot hurt to acquire arts and skills that may prove useful. I am campaigning my father to be allowed to learn how to load and fire a musket. Perhaps with my newfound skill at the legerdemain, I shall be able to discharge a weapon in the blinking of an eye.

Respectfully yours,

Amelia Hornsby

Amelia Hornsby, Magician

P.S. I shall await the publication of your inaugural address, and I wish you many felicitations for the ceremony.

Bridge over the Schuylkill River, Philadelphia

To learn more about 19th century newspapers, visit winslowpress.com.

To learn more about entertainment in the 1800s, visit winslowpress.com.

Washington City

Dear Miss Amelia,

It is with the greatest delight and enthusiasm that I inform you of our first report from Captain Lewis. In April, he dispatched an account some 45,000 words long from their winter camp at Fort Mandan, among the Hidatsa people, and it has lately arrived here.

Along with the report he sent 108 botanical specimens accompanied by labels expressing the days on which obtained, places found, and also their verities and properties when known; also crates of earth, salts, and minerals; also the skeletons of male and female antelopes of a heretofore undescribed species; also preserved insects, mice, animal skins including skins of the mighty buffalo; also live specimens of a number of animals until now unknown to science! These being a kind of magpie and a rodent like unto a marmot that Lewis describes as a "prairie dog." He says this animal lives in great colonies underground, some of these colonies stretching over many miles of land. Further wonders of the animal world include vast flocks of Carolina parrot queets at the mouth of the Kansas River; as well as a flock of white pelicans three miles long floating down the Missouri. These marvels are almost too astonishing to credit; and yet credit them we must!

Of inexpressible value also is the map, which by dint of careful surveying at every opportunity by the company, shows the route of the Mississippi and Missouri Rivers, with each encampment duly noted. Experimentation with the botanical specimens may discover to our scientists that several thereof may with great value be introduced into cultivation; it will therefore be possible to ascertain by cross-referencing this map with the specimen labels where and under what circumstances the plant was found. The majority of these specimens have already been forwarded to

To learn more about the animals discovered by Lewis and Clark, visit winslowpress.com.

Hall of the Academy of Natural Sciences, Philadelphia, which Amelia sometimes visited. Engraving by Fenner, Sears, & Co. from drawing by Burton in History by I.T. Hinton, 1830.

the American Philosophical Society. And you can be certain that your former guardian, Dr. Rush, and his learned colleagues, are turning their intellects to these new products of the interior. The zoological specimens have, by and large, been delivered to Mr. Peale. I fear you will regret having departed Philadelphia before the arrival of these prodigies. There were also numerous artifacts of the various Indian nations encountered, for example Mandan, Minittarra, Hidatsa, Ahwahharway, and Arikara.

If you have been faithful in your weather recording, you may compare Pittsburgh's winter temperature with Fort Mandan's: Capt. Lewis says the Mercury dropped lower than 20 degrees below zero more than once. They spent their idle months of winter encampment improving the quality of their clothing, which in Indian fashion is made of animal hides, this being the most effective means of preserving warmth.

Of all Lewis's news, I think you may find this among the most interesting: in November of last year, they took into the company a young Indian woman of the Shoshoni tribe. She is but fifteen years old and married to a Frenchman named Charbonneau. Her native home is west of the great Rocky Mountains, which is precisely where Lewis and Clark aim to go. This maiden, whose name is Sacagawea, will guide them there. In February she gave birth to her first child; he is a boy named by his father, Jean Baptiste. Sacagawea will lead the company to the Pacific Ocean with this infant on her back.

If you can credit such an extraordinary turn of events, a young woman scarce older than yourself is now the principal guide of the Corps of Discovery.

Your humble servant,

Th. Jefferson

October 12, 1805

Pittsburgh

To Mr. Th. Jefferson, President

Washington City

Dear Sir,

This report of the Indian guide Sacagawea is indeed astonishing news. I do not say astonishing that a young woman should be capable of such a task. Rather, I find it astonishing that the captains should allow themselves to be guided by a female. The captains seem all the more remarkable to me on account of it. They show themselves to be a great deal more liberal-minded than the majority of men, and I mean specifically my cousin Josiah Hornsby of the Baltimore Hornsbys who refuses to teach me how to ride a horse astride. He says it is unseemly for a young woman to acquire such manly skills as shooting and riding, learning Greek, understanding the operation of a compass and sextant, or in fact, anything that is stimulating and interesting to a person of intellect living at the raw edge of civilization. When I informed him that the Corps of Discovery was now under the guidance of a woman—and a young woman but one year my senior—he said that being an Indian, Sacagawea does not count.

Now, sir, I do not think that he can be correct in this statement. In Philadelphia, I did often follow with great interest the activities of the Free Africa Society, organized there by the Rev. Absolom Jones of St. George's Methodist Episcopal Church, and read his opinions and often heard him speak. It became quite clear to me that little difference other than the most superficial lies between the races of Caucasian and Ethiopian. If no true difference exists between these two races, then why are we to assume a different case for the Indian? If the difference in condition or station is due only to lack of education on the one hand, or greater material wealth on the other, then we may suppose that Sacagawea is no different from myself. My logic is not to be challenged, I think, and my second cousin Josiah Hornsby of the Baltimore Hornsbys is talking nonsense every time he opens his mouth on the subject.

Please, if you would, let me know more of the report you had from Captain Lewis, especially those parts that touch on Sacagawea. My small circle of friends, the girls who see me as such a font of all wisdom, are as anxious as I am to hear more about this Indian guide.

Respectfully yours,

Amelia Hornsby

Amelia Hornsby, Reformer

To learn more about Sacagawea, visit winslowpress.com.

To learn more about the Free Africa Society, visit winslowpress.com.

Old compass

61

December 3, 1805

Washington City

Dear Miss Hornsby,

You beg for more information on the Indian guide, Sacagawea, and I will happily oblige to the best of my ability. But before I do so, I venture to ask if you had heard report of the remarkable *Orukter Amphibolis* demonstrated at Philadelphia some months ago. Recalling your fascination with strange and wonderful new vehicles, I wish to assure myself that you knew of this device. If this report describes what you already know, I beg your pardon, but I dare not take that chance that it is unknown to you.

Oliver Evans of Philadelphia, an inventor of considerable skill, mounted a steam-powered dredge onto a carriage. By connecting the moving parts of the steam engine to the wheels of the carriage, he was able to drive this *Orukter Amphibolis*, as he dubbed it, around Center Square and out Market Street to the Schuylkill. At this point he transferred the power to especially fashioned water propulsion wheels and navigated this wondrous machine down the Schuylkill and out to the Delaware, where he drove it up and down for some time, to the delight and astonishment of the citizens of Philadelphia who made their observations from the wharves. I feel sure that if you had still resided in that city, you would have been at the front of the crowd.

Inventions of this sort are a great fascination of mine; I regret I was not able to witness this demonstration myself. News of it was published in several journals, and I also had report of it from my friends at the Philosophical Society.

To learn more about Oliver Evans and the *Orukter Amphibolis*, visit winslowpress.com.

The *Orukter Amphibolis*

Mr. Charles Willson Peale was particularly enthralled with the device.

I have been able to introduce several inventions of mine own into practice at my home in Monticello. One of which I am particularly proud is the clock in the entrance hall which can be read from inside and outside; in addition, the weights, which by means of gravity drive the clock mechanism, indicate the days of the week on the interior wall of the hall as they descend. I also designed a cunning mechanism which allows both panels of a double door to open in unison when only one is touched. If only I had more time to devote to ingenious plans of this sort! Indeed, my longings for retirement are so strong, that I with difficulty encounter the daily drudgeries of my duty; and that duty keeps me at the capital much more than I could wish.

Now, to your question over the Indian guide. Sadly, Lewis reported little more than what I have already described. Sacagawea is one of two squaws, or wives, of this French trader Toussaint Charbonneau, whom the Corps encountered at Fort Mandan. This man has lived among the Hidatsa for some time and speaks their tongue quite passably well. His younger squaw is this Sacagawea. She is a native of the Shoshoni, or Snake, tribe from the country west of the mountains,

and was captured by the Hidatsas during a hunting expedition when she was quite young; and was raised from that time among the Hidatsas. Lewis says her name means Bird Woman in the Hidatsa tongue; but as she is not by birth a Hidatsa, perhaps her name has a different import in the language of the Snake. Her knowledge of the upper waters of the Missouri, its tributaries and rapids, will be of vital importance to the company.

Upon meeting this Sacagawea, Lewis observed that she was with child. It was he himself who assisted her in her delivery in February; and as it was her first labor, it was long and tedious; being told by some other person (Indian or American, I know not) that the rattle of a snake was known to ease the pains of childbirth, he mixed some pieces with water and bade her drink. Lewis says he knows not if this be the cause, but within minutes she had brought forth her infant, Jean Baptiste.

As of the time Lewis prepared his report to me, he said that when they resumed their journey, they would be sleeping in Indian tents known as tepees; these being of conical shape and made of dressed buffalo hide; and Sacagawea made these.

Further, Lewis reported that all in the company were in excellent health and good spirits, all zealously attached to the enterprise still before them. Clark's servant, York, excites much interest among the natives by virtue of the blackness of his skin, but they do not fear him or believe him a threat and for that I know the party are thankful. We shall not know until their return if this woman Sacagawea can lead them to the

To learn more about York, visit winslowpress.com.

Background: "Lewis and Clark's Trail" reproduced by Robert Vaughn, 1905. Right: Lieutenant Zebulon Pike

great salt ocean. But time may prove to us that even as I write this letter, my friend Lewis is casting his gaze upon the Pacific waters, having penetrated the continent to its extreme edge.

Your humble servant,

Th. Jefferson

P.S. We also await news from Lt. Zebulon Pike, who is making the ascent of the Mississippi River to its source. I feel very much the truth of the parable of casting my bread upon the waters; I do not doubt it will return a thousandfold.

January 5, 1806

Pittsburgh

Dear Sir,

I pray you are right when you express the hope that the Corps of Discovery has already achieved the ocean; and I add this prayer to yours: that Sacagawea will return with them to claim her portion of the honor that is due to them.

My father and my second cousin Josiah Hornsby of the Baltimore Hornsbys have lately received several back numbers of the Philadelphia papers. They are full of news of the specimens sent by Lewis, and which Mr. Peale and Mr. Hamilton and Dr. Benjamin Smith Barton and others are busy studying. I know that as president of the American Philosophical Society you are well aware of the progress of these examinations.

But I feel such a fever of curiosity that I cannot help but speculate on paper. Dr. Barton intends to create the botanical catalog himself, I hear; his Flora Missourica will be much anticipated.

And how I regret not being in Philadelphia now to see the little prairie dog and the magpie that now make their home at Independence Hall! They are messengers from the interior, if only we knew how to interpret their language! I understand that Dr. Barton is taking a particular interest in their well-being. If only these animals could be sensible of the honor being paid to them, for they have been and continue to be the special charges of some of the greatest men in this country!

My father says I may make a visit to Philadelphia in the springtime; and when I do, I shall not fail to visit these famous travelers; until the men who sent them return, these are the next best thing.

Respectfully yours,

Amelia Hornsby

Amelia Hornsby, Exile

Portrait of Charles Willson Peale

Refurbished entrance hall of American Philosophical Society, photo by Y.D. Hubbard. Inset: Exterior of American Philosophical Society, photo by Y.D. Hubbard

Washington City

Dear Miss Hornsby,

You sound somewhat melancholic, and for that I send you this for consolation, a paraphrase of the Roman poet, Ovid, who said that he who runs changes his sky, not his heart. Only I imagine it is precisely that which you wish to change. Pittsburgh must be very dull compared to the stimulation of Philadelphia. In the event you do make a visit to that city, I shall recommend to my colleagues at the Philosophical Society to treat you as an honored guest.

At home, by which I mean Monticello, we are beginning to put in a new road to the top of the mount; in good weather this should give us faster access to the house. You see that I, too, wish to change my sky. I want very much to be at home, with my grandchildren about me and my vegetable gardens to visit. If I were at home now I would be watching eagerly for the first shoots of the spring pea, my very favorite vegetable. This is a dangerous month, when spring shows to us so many enchanting signals of her approach; and yet when the vengeful winter may still lash at us with its last cruel claws. Last week, my daughter reported that the cherries and peaches were in bloom. Now the flowers have all been killed by a late frost, and I despair of having cherry and peach pies this summer when the government is in recess and I can go home.

We're neither one of us where we wish to be, my young friend; our duties take precedence over our desires.

Your humble servant,

Th. Jefferson

Front of Monticello, photo by Theodor Horydczak

May 25, 1806

Philadelphia
To Mr. Thomas Jefferson, President
Washington City

Dear Sir,

I write to you from the home of my dear friend, Dr. Rush, who sends you greetings. My dear father allowed me to make this visit, and I have traveled here in the company of my cousin, Josiah Hornsby.

You can be sure that my first order of business upon my return was to visit Mr. Peale's Museum to see the dear prairie dog and magpie, who are such celebrated aliens in this city. They seem both to be thriving, even in the glare of public attention. I have also been privileged to examine many of the other artifacts and specimens sent back here by Captain Lewis, and to that I believe I am indebted to you, sir. Both Dr. Barton and Dr. Rush made remarks to wit: that a certain highly placed gentleman now residing at Washington had made an especial request that I be shown these marvels. Thank you.

I can hardly believe the evidence of my own eyes when I observe this city: so much has changed in the more than one year I have been absent. How busy it is by comparison to Pittsburgh! I cannot have become utterly rusticated. This city is certainly more bustling than ever it was. Now that there is a bridge across the Delaware at Trenton, it is possible to travel by coach from Philadelphia to the edge of the Hudson across from Manhattan. And it seems to me that there is a great deal more coach and horse traffic now as a result. As soon as there is a bridge across the Hudson River, one will be able to travel from Manhattan to Philadelphia

To learn more about Philadelphia, visit winslowpress.com.

The famous Peale Museum was originally located in Peale's house at Third and Lombard Streets, Philadelphia.

without pause. This leads my wandering imagination to further ruminations on the Corps of Discovery: perhaps we will soon be able to travel clear across the continent from the Atlantic to the Pacific. That will be a great marvel indeed.

Respectfully yours,

Amelia Hornsby

Amelia Hornsby, Visionary

Pittsburgh

Dear Miss Hornsby,

You will, I know, exult in my news. I have yesterday received word from Capt. Lewis. A letter, forwarded on from Saint Louis, announces their safe return. Indeed, the Corps of Discovery reached the Pacific Ocean late last fall, and wintered there, leaving that place on 26th March. They accomplished their return to Saint Louis in September this year; with Capt. Lewis wounded although recovering swiftly. He will join us here in Washington City as soon as able.

Pressing business prevents me from adding more at this time.

Your humble servant,

Th. Jefferson

P.S. October 26—I kept this letter open, in the hope that I might find time to add more of those details which I know will interest you. Although many triumphs attended their journey, Capt. Lewis had the sad duty to inform me that no true Northwest Passage exists. He writes that they have discovered the most practicable route which does exist across the continent by means of the navigable branches of the Missouri and Columbia Rivers; and that the rivers of the west are in large part naviga-ble; but that the passage by land from the Missouri to the Columbia is a terrible ordeal which makes the route impracticable. Thus we must con-clude for now that no all-water passage connects our two oceans, and one of the primary goals of this expedition is unmet.
T. J.

Early etching of Meriwether Lewis

Pittsburgh
To Mr. Thomas Jefferson, President
Washington City

Dear Sir,

We have by now read many of the reports ourselves, as they have been published in the *Gazette*. Of much interest here at Pittsburgh was the news, brought to us by a member of this college, of having attended the public auction in Saint Louis where Captains Lewis and Clark sold off so many of the items employed on their tour. This colleague of my father's, one Landau Herrick, bought for himself the rifle carried by Pvt. Cruzatte; and as we understand, it was this rifle by which Capt. Lewis was accidentally shot and wounded. It is a souvenir of considerable value to Mr. Herrick and of interest to us all.

We will be very eager to know if Capts. Lewis and Clark and their entourage will be stopping at Pittsburgh. The news informs us that they make very slow progress indeed, as they are stopped at every town and settlement and hailed as returning heroes. I imagine they will be heartily sick of balls and banquets before they take another step. Yet if they do come to Pittsburgh, we shall not fail to celebrate these titans of exploration.

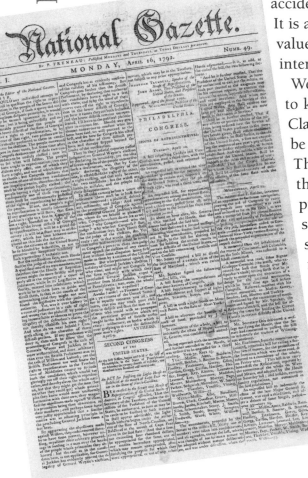

How sorry I was to learn that Sacagawea must stay with her husband, Charbonneau, with the Mandan. What puzzles me is the report that Charbonneau was paid in excess of $500 for his services to the Corps of Discovery; but nowhere have I found a report of any payment rendered to Sacagawea. I should be most interested to hear at what value her services were placed. For inasmuch as she did most swiftly and expertly guide the company across the Rocky Mountains and to the Columbia River, thence to the sea, her services would seem invaluable.

And inasmuch as I must consider some employment for myself beyond being my father's hostess (for he is to marry a widow lady of this town), I should like to know how highly a woman might be compensated for hard work. I do not propose that I should be a wilderness guide. But it has been suggested to me that a person of my education and attainments might do well as a teacher for young ladies; and as this suits my temper very well, I think I may try it when I am of suitable years.

Respectfully yours,

Amelia Hornsby

Amelia Hornsby, Educator

P.S. I hope that the Negro slave York was not also denied his fair portion of reward?
A. H.

The National Gazette *was published in Philadelphia as early as 1792.*

To learn more about the role of women in the 1800s, visit winslowpress.com.

Washington
To Miss Amelia Hornsby
Pittsburgh

Dear Miss Hornsby,

I can say that January 1, 1807, will always be a signal day in my memories; for Capt. Lewis met with me here at the Executive Mansion, and we conversed from morning into the darkest hours of the night; and he will remain here through the winter, telling me all. My head is filled with the marvelous tales he has brought back from his epic journey. Where shall I begin in relating to you the most notable events of his tale?

Let me begin by reporting on the delegation of Indians which traveled with Lewis. On the 30th of December we first received the members of the Osage tribe with much ceremony and exchange of gifts; then on the following day was our audience with the Mandan ambassadors, and with their chief, Big White. They dress in their own curious fashion; and they were highly sensible of the pomp and formality of the occasion to meet their "Big Father." It is my devoutest wish to initiate commerce with these people with all good will; and if it be possible, to turn them away from their nomadic habits and attempt to situate them on farming settlements.

Capt. Lewis shared with me many remarkable stories of his relations with them; and further described the wonders of the great American West. He related many hair-raising incidents with the grizzly bear, which is larger and more ferocious than any bear here in the East; and which by virtue of its very great size and strength, has little to fear from man. As he speaks I see before me the great pinnacled rocks, and hear the thunderous voice of the Great Falls of the Missouri and the many impetuous cataracts that impeded their progress. My own heart leapt with joy as he recounted the unexpected reunion of Sacagawea with her brother and her former friends among the Shoshoni in the Bitterroot Mountains. On the return journey, the party split in two; while Clark led one company to explore the Yellowstone River, Lewis took another to investigate the Marias River to the north. Their reunion in August was a day of celebration in the wilderness.

Truly, there is too much to hear and to say between myself and Capt. Lewis. It is our hope that very soon excerpts from his journals will be published to the amazement and edification of all the world. And I pray you will excuse me from repeating all that my friend has told me, as you will soon enough be able to read it in its fullest detail yourself.

Yr. humble servant,

Thos. Jefferson

February 29, 1807

Pittsburgh
To Mr. Thomas Jefferson, President
Executive Mansion, Washington

Dear Sir,

    This is indeed strange news about Mr. Burr. Can he truly have headed a conspiracy to form a new nation combining Mexico and parts of the Louisiana Territory? It strikes me as extremely odd. You must know him well; can these reports have any merit? It is terribly difficult to understand world events here in our backwater; without the company of so many learned people as we were used to in Philadelphia, our debates run round and round in circles of futility. We know not what to make of Napoleon's activities abroad, for example. And how important is it that Britain prohibits neutral nations from trading with France? Surely they can have no authority over the United States? Sir, we are at a loss to fathom how the disturbances in Europe should touch upon us.

    I find these brief though wondrous accounts of Capts. Lewis and Clark far less strange than the agitations of the Europeans. If you can assist me in making sense of these developments, I shall endeavor to explain them to my young protegés.

Respectfully yrs,

Amelia Hornsby

Amelia Hornsby, Perplexed

To learn more about Aaron Burr, visit winslowpress.com.

Etching of Aaron Burr

Washington City
To Miss Amelia Hornsby
Pittsburgh

Dear Miss Amelia,

What is at stake here is the freedom of the seas; enmity between France and Britain should have no bearing on us, being neutral. But if our ships are molested upon the high seas, this would be cause for grave concern. There are many subtle characteristics to the question, but that is it in a nutshell. I find it vexing in the extreme that just when we would most wish to turn our attention inward and westward, taking into account our newly explored territories and all that we may discover there, that we are being plagued by the threadbare nuisances of an exhausted Old World.

Yr. humble servant,

Th: Jefferson

Thos. Jefferson

P.S. And I should gladly see Burr convicted of treason.

Pittsburgh

To Mr. Thos. Jefferson
Washington City

Dear Sir,

You will be interested to hear what effect Capt. Lewis's reports are having here on the frontier. News that those fur-bearing creatures, namely the otter and the beaver, live in unparalleled abundance in the lands of the upper Missouri and its branches, has generated an enthusiasm to be marveled at. Not a conversation takes place without reference to the anticipated fur trade, and the vast fortunes to be made at it. We know three men (I do not say gentlemen, you will see why) who have abandoned their families to go west for trapping.

One of these wastrels is the father of one of my small friends; there is very little I can do to console one who has been forsaken in this heartless way. The family is thrown upon charity in the father's absence; indeed, we speculate on the likelihood of his ever returning.

Is this not a most unexpected consequence of this extraordinary journey?

Sincerely yours,

Amelia Hornsby

Amelia Hornsby, Defender of Outcasts

Portrait of Aaron Burr at about age 25   *Etching of an otter*

Monticello
To Miss Amelia Hornsby, Pittsburgh

Dear Miss Hornsby,

I am truly grieved at your young friend's loss; but it is the duty of every father to provide for his children. And if he saw no other recourse than to abandon them in this way, I can only say that I have often been compelled to do the same. Often and oftener, my obligations have parted me from my beloved ones. We must pray always that those who now venture into these territories will be blessed by good fortune, as were Capts. Lewis and Clark.

I can only offer this, which may be very small consolation to your friend: that opening the continent for commerce was one of the principle objectives of the Corps of Discovery. We cannot expect profit without an expense of effort and the sacrifice of what might have been happy days at home.

Indeed, we gain little by shirking from difficult or daunting tasks.

Even now, I fear that our sacrifices on behalf of liberty will have to be renewed. But we would not be the country we are now had we balked in earlier days. We must not let love of comfort and coziness prevent us from doing what we must.

Your humble servant,

Thos. Jefferson

Detail of portrait of Thomas Jefferson

To learn more about relations between England and the United States, visit winslowpress.com.

Pittsburgh
To Mr. Thomas Jefferson, President
Washington City

Dear Sir,

This is an outrage! I think you are quite correct to close our American ports to armed British vessels. That an American ship should be halted on the high seas and some of her crew impressed—it is unspeakable. The British perhaps did not learn to leave US (I mean United States) alone. If I still lived in Philadelphia, sir, I would be on the wharves myself with my muscat, to fend off these pirates, the so-called British Navy.

I have taken to heart what you last wrote me; liberty is worthy of any sacrifice. But I believe we denigrate liberty if we make the self-same sacrifice for profit.

Respectfully yrs,

Amelia Hornsby

Amelia Hornsby, Patriot

P.S. I am curious to know if you have sampled this carbonated water I have read of in the *Gazette*. I have often tasted naturally fizzled water, but this is produced by a chemical process.
A. H.

P.P.S. Please give my regards to Capt. Lewis if he is yet in the capital. I am sure he must remember me.
A. H.

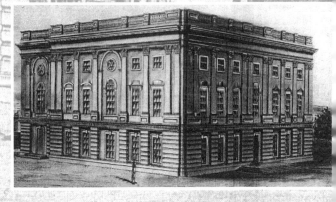

The Capitol, 1803

Monticello

Dear Miss Hornsby

Since your last letter Washington has been in a tumult; Burr's trial in Richmond was very much on my mind throughout August. And relations with Britain are worsening. Politics makes an assault on my senses day and night. Now that I am home at Monticello, it is only with the greatest effort of will that I imagine returning to the fray.

I am once again sympathetic to your wearisome exile from Philadelphia; Captain Lewis was there for the greater part of the summer. He was busy with the Philosophical Society, giving his report in great detail; and you can well speculate how much I would rather have been there than at the capital.

Lewis is now on his way to Saint Louis, where he will reside as governor of the Territory of Louisiana. I can think of no one better suited to the job. Perhaps he will pause for some time at Pittsburgh, affording you the opportunity to ask him your many questions about Sacagawea. But you can be confident in knowing that his journals and notes and maps are being prepared for publication as soon as is possible. My daily activities seem to be nothing but a tedium when cast into shadow by the exploits of those heroic men.

I toured my fruit gardens this morning, with an eye toward the progress of my cider crop. I am really only a farmer, at the end of the day. I think I shall take a walk down my Mulberry Row before I retire this night, and look out toward the west. Perhaps if the wind is still I shall catch a faint echo from the far, faraway ocean.

Yr. humble servant,

Thomas Jefferson

Detail of etching of Thomas Jefferson

Monticello, photo by John Collier, 1913. Background: A description by a guest named Judith Lomax of clouds covering a mountain near Monticello, from one of Jefferson's journals

Pittsburgh

Dear Sir,

It grieves me to hear a disconsolate tone in your last letter to me. If you will forgive a familiarity on my part, I say, for shame, sir, to be downhearted! Perhaps, as your letter was written three months ago, your melancholic humor has been allayed. This is the season of the Nativity, when thoughts of our divine Savior fill our hearts with hope; and as tonight is the winter solstice, we may awake tomorrow to the prospect of longer and fairer days ahead. Cast off your gloom, sir! Be joyful! Life is renewed!

How can you not be uplifted when you contemplate the magnificent discoveries of Capts. Lewis and Clark? I recall to you your wish to prove (to certain doubters in Europe) that North American fauna are not feeble and degenerate. I say show to them the grizzly bear! Surely no such terrible creature dwells in the old world. True, no behemoths were found living. But what of the mammoth tusk fossils unearthed at Big Bone Lick?

Or the lesser, though no more degenerate animals such as the mountain goat, the pocket gopher, the prodigious mountain lion or the bobcat? And the unnumbered plants, whose uses may yet be found to heal the sick or feed the hungry? The mind reels at the prospect of seeing the lofty spruces of the Northwest. I think the old world can have little to compete with such mighty forest giants as that!

To my imagination, it is comparable to hearing a waterfall in the dark, and then having the sun arise and reveal the splendors of the cataract more glorious than any dreaming. In just such a manner have the intrepid explorers brought to our senses riches and wonders of this continent past our capacity to invent. And you it was who sent them there. For this I thank you with the humblest gratitude.

Sincerely,

Amelia Hornsby

Amelia Hornsby, Devoted Friend

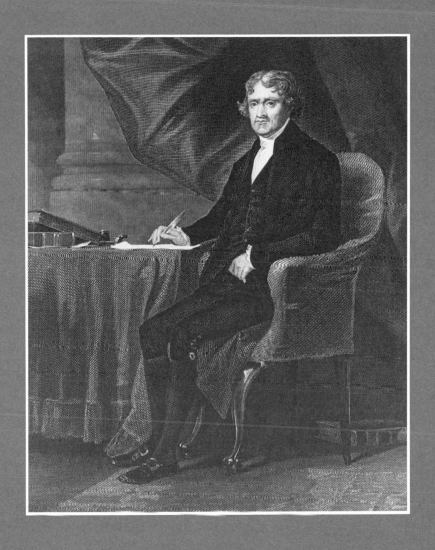

MESSAGE

FROM THE

PRESIDENT OF THE UNITED STATES,

COMMUNICATING

DISCOVERIES

MADE IN EXPLORING

THE MISSOURI, RED RIVER AND WASHITA,

BY

CAPTAINS LEWIS AND CLARK, DOCTOR SIBLEY,

AND

MR. DUNBAR;

WITH

A STATISTICAL ACCOUNT

OF THE

COUNTRIES ADJACENT.

FEBRUARY 19, 1806.

Read, and ordered to lie on the table.

CITY OF WASHINGTON:

A. & G. WAY, PRINTERS.

....

1806.

Copy 1

Thomas Jefferson kept careful records of the discoveries made by Lewis and Clark.

The Young Thomas Jefferson

Thomas Jefferson was born in Virginia on April 13, 1743. His father, Colonel Peter Jefferson, was a landowner and local justice of the peace. He was also a skilled surveyor and mapmaker. His mother, Jane Randolph, came from an influential and wealthy Virginia family.

For the first few years of Jefferson's life, the family lived at Shadwell Plantation in Albermarle County (then known as Goochland County). He was the third of ten children—he had six sisters and three brothers. Two of his siblings died before they reached adulthood.

At about three years old, Thomas moved with his parents to Tuckahoe Plantation, where they would live for the next six years. Tuckahoe had been owned by William Randolph, a good friend of Peter Jefferson's. When Randolph died, Thomas's father took over the management of the plantation. He also took responsibility for raising Randolph's children. The Jeffersons returned to Shadwell when Thomas was nine years old.

Jefferson said that the move to Tuckahoe was his earliest memory. He remembered riding on horseback with one of the family's slaves, a large pillow tucked beneath him to protect him from the bumpy ride.

We do not know a great deal about Thomas Jefferson's childhood. He wrote very little about it in *Autobiography*, and any records or journals of his early life were destroyed by a

Member of the Continental Congress in Philadelphia, where he completed the initial draft of the Declaration of Independence

Member of the Virginia House of Delegates

Daughter Maria "Polly" born

Governor of Virginia

fire at Shadwell in 1770. However, we know that Thomas was a quiet, curious boy with a consuming interest in observing and recording the details of the world around him. He spent hours in the forests and mountains that surrounded his Virginia homes, watching and learning about the plants and animals that he found there.

When he was nine years old, Jefferson was sent to Northam, Virginia, to study with the Reverend Douglas, a clergyman. The school was so far from home that Thomas boarded with Reverend Douglas, coming back to his family for just part of each year. Jefferson would later write that his teacher was "a superficial Latinist, less instructed in Greek, but with the rudiments of these languages he taught me French." He seems to have been bored and unhappy at the school, and he missed his home.

Peter Jefferson died when Thomas was fourteen. The loss of his father, whom he admired greatly, was a real blow to him. He left Reverend Douglas's school and enrolled in the Reverend James Maury's school, which was twelve miles from Shadwell— close enough that he could come home every weekend.

James Maury had a personal library of more than four hundred books. This was quite large by the standards of Colonial America, since books were expensive and sometimes difficult to obtain. Thomas spent much of his time devouring the books in the schoolmaster's library; he also took dancing lessons and studied the violin.

Just before his seventeenth birthday, Jefferson entered the

1782

Martha Jefferson
dies at Monticello

1783–1784

Member of the
Continental Congress at
Annapolis, the tempo-
rary capital

1785–1789

U.S. minister to
France

College of William and Mary in Williamsburg, Virginia. He
attended the philosophy school and studied mathematics and
science with Dr. William Small, whose teaching "probably
fixed the destinies of my life," he wrote years later. Dr. Small
introduced Jefferson to the sciences, which became another
of the future president's passions.

Although he was a disciplined student, he had a busy social
life. He belonged to a "social fraternity" called the Flat Hat
Club. The club, Jefferson said years later, "had no useful
object." Jefferson and his friends also enjoyed long dinners at
which they talked about law, politics, and philosophy. Those
dinners *did* have a "useful object." To them, he "owed much
instruction."

Career

Thomas Jefferson went on to study law, pass the bar exam
to become a lawyer, and become a member of the House of
Burgesses, Virginia's legislature, while still in his twenties.
He objected to the British Parliament's authority over the
colonies and the fact that the colonists had to obey British
laws even though they had no vote. Jefferson was also angered
by the religious intolerance encouraged by the British. It
was his belief that all forms of religious worship should be
tolerated. He became active in an underground group that
had links to rebels in other colonies.

1790–1793   1797–1801   1801–1809

U.S. secretary of   Vice president of the   President of the
state   United States under   United States
                             President John Adams

Jefferson also supported efforts in the legislature to emancipate Virginia's slaves. The effort failed, which did not seem to have surprised him. "Nothing liberal could expect success" under British government, he wrote in *Autobiography*. Jefferson himself owned slaves, and would continue to do so for the rest of his life. This is one of the contradictions of his personality that historians have been puzzling and arguing over for many years—even to this day. There is even DNA evidence that Thomas Jefferson could have been the father of one of the sons of a slave named Sally Hemings who worked at Monticello.

Jefferson became a member of the Continental Congress in 1775. The Congress first met in 1774—it was a group of representatives from all the colonies, and its mission was to draw up a framework of "common measures" binding the colonies together. Jefferson was appointed to the committee responsible for drafting a declaration of independence from Britain. John Adams, Benjamin Franklin, and the other members of the committee decided that Jefferson was the best qualified to write the draft because of his eloquence and writing style. Thus, Thomas Jefferson is known to us as the author of the Declaration of Independence.

In the fall of 1776, while America was fighting Britain for its independence, Jefferson left the Continental Congress in Philadelphia and returned to Virginia. He was a member of the Virginia House of Delegates (which succeeded the House of Burgesses) until 1779, when he became governor of the state. Eventually, he would serve as the new nation's minister

1803

The Louisiana
Purchase occurs

Lewis and Clark's
Trail

Words and Music by Robert Vaughn

Robert Vaughn
Great Falls, Montana

1803–1806

The Lewis and Clark
expedition

to France and then as its secretary of state before being
elected John Adams's vice president.

In those days, a presidential candidate didn't choose a
running mate—instead, the candidate who won the second
highest number of votes in the election became the vice
president, while the candidate who won the highest number
of votes won the presidency. In 1796, Jefferson ran against
John Adams for the presidency and came in second. Thus, he
became the vice president. In 1800, Republican congressional
caucus chose Jefferson to run for the presidency against John
Adams, who belonged to the Federalist Party.

It was a bitter, personal campaign between the two men and
much of it revolved around the two parties' different views on
federal authority and the rights of individual states. Put very
simply, the Republicans believed that individual states should
have a certain amount of independence; the less interference
by the federal government the better. The Federalists, on the
other hand, believed that power should be centralized in the
federal government. Jefferson beat Adams by a narrow margin
but tied with Aaron Burr. Because of the tie, the election
was sent to the House of Representatives to be decided.
The Federalist-controlled House preferred Jefferson to Burr
and, in 1801, he was inaugurated as the third president of
the United States.

1804

1807

1808

Daughter Polly
Jefferson Eppes dies
at the age of twenty-
five on April 17

Aaron Burr, on
the run, is cap-
tured and tried
for treason

James Madison elected
president

The Presidential Years

In 1803, the United States purchased the Louisiana Territory
from France. Though President Jefferson and his negotiators,
Robert L. Livingston and James Monroe (later our fifth
president), had planned to buy a much smaller area, Napoleon
made a surprise offer of the whole territory. The French no
longer felt the need to reestablish a hold in North America.
Napoleon's brother-in-law, Victor Leclerc, had failed in an
initial mission to do just that.

France's territory on St. Domingue (the western half of
the island now comprising the countries of Haiti and the
Dominican Republic) had been wrested from its control by
civil wars and slave uprisings. By 1803 it was what one historian
has called "a de facto black republic" led by General Toussaint
l'Ouverture. As an initial step in his plan to regain control of
territories in North America, Napoleon sent Leclerc on a
mission to subdue the slaves. The mission failed miserably,
with 20,000 French soldiers lost to yellow fever and guerilla
warfare. Leclerc himself died, and the failure of this ambitious
expedition played a part in changing Napoleon's mind about
holding on to the Louisiana Territory. Napoleon was also on
the verge of war with Britain, and his country needed the
cash that selling the territory would bring.

This huge Territory between the Mississippi River and the
Rockies included the present-day states of Louisiana, Arkansas,
Missouri, Iowa, Minnesota, North and South Dakota, Nebraska,

Kansas, Oklahoma, Texas, New Mexico, Colorado, Wyoming, and Montana.

Exploration of the western part of North America had long been an obsession of Jefferson's. As a child, he had been impressed by his father's skills and achievements as a mapmaker and surveyor, and since then he had been fascinated by exploration and explorers. His obsession with Western exploration was fed by his many interests (such as natural history, geography and mapmaking, astronomy, agriculture, and language, to name a few).

In 1802, before the purchase, Jefferson had asked the Spanish minister in Washington if it would be all right with his government for the United States Congress to authorize exploration of the Missouri River. His main interest was in mapping the course of the river and learning about the plant and animal life of the territory, the climate and geography, and the Native-American tribes who inhabited the region. However, he told Congress that the expedition would have money-making potential. Jefferson knew that Congress would never be able to authorize funding for an expedition being launched out of sheer curiosity. There had to be an economic benefit to the country.

The Spanish government was unsure of Jefferson's motives, but Jefferson took his project into the planning phase anyway, asking Congress for money to explore the Missouri River and discover its source. Congress approved the president's request for funds, and when the approval came through, Jefferson was

1826

Thomas Jefferson
dies on July 4, the
fiftieth anniversary
of the Declaration
of Independence

prepared. He had been readying his secretary, Meriwether
Lewis, to lead the expedition, which was officially formed
near the end of 1803.

In his first term as president, Thomas Jefferson was quite
popular. The Louisiana Purchase was a major achievement,
doubling the size of the United States. In addition, Jefferson
cut the budget and reduced the country's national debt. It
was then that pirates roaming the Mediterranean began to
cause trouble for the new Republic.

The pirates of North Africa's Barbary States had been taking
advantage of ships traveling through the Mediterranean Sea.
They attacked and looted ships, and were so feared that the
United States and other countries preferred to pay them
"protection" money rather than fight back. However,
Jefferson opposed this on principle. He didn't believe that
the Americans should have to pay protection money to the
Barbary pirates just so they could sail their ships through the
Mediterranean in peace. When the pirates of Tripoli demanded
more money in 1801, Jefferson refused, and Tripoli declared
war on the United States.

Over the next few years, the American Navy fought battles
off the Tripoli coast, which is in present day Libya. An
American ship, the *Philadelphia*, was seized by pirates and used
to attack other U.S. ships. Jefferson sent most of the U.S.
fleet to the Mediterranean, but the pirates burned down the
Philadelphia and held her captain and crew hostage for nearly
two years. Although the Barbary pirates finally agreed to stop
demanding protection money from the Americans, Jefferson

was still forced to pay a large ransom for the *Philadelphia*'s crew.

Thomas Jefferson's second term was less successful than his first. One reason for this was the political effect of the Burr Conspiracy, in which Aaron Burr, his former vice president, was put on trial for treason. Jefferson made the mistake of publicly declaring Burr's guilt even before the trial had taken place, thus alienating Burr's supporters. Another reason for Jefferson's declining popularity was the embargo adopted by the U.S. in December of 1807.

American business was caught in the middle of the fighting between the French and the British in the Napoleonic Wars. Jefferson refused to take sides and engage the country in a war with these two powers. Instead, he decided to suspend trade with both countries. The embargo prohibited all exports to Britain and France. Unfortunately, it caused great economic problems for the Americans, while having little effect on the British and French. Enforcing the unpopular Embargo meant that the government could not act according to many of Jefferson's own principles. Close to the end of his term, the president finally agreed to end the Embargo, but he left office having lost the support of some of the people who had backed him.

Home and Family

During his five years in the House of Burgesses, Thomas Jefferson married Martha Wayles Skelton, a young widow, whom he probably met in Williamsburg. We know little about her, but according to her great-granddaughter Sarah Randolph, she was well educated for a woman of that time, and a "constant reader." Martha was also musically talented, which may have been part of her attraction to Jefferson. She and Jefferson often played duets, Martha on the harpsichord and Thomas on the violin.

By the time he was married, he had already begun building his dream home, Monticello, but it would be years before the house was finished. Even before he cleared the Virginia mountaintop for building, Jefferson had begun keeping his garden books, in which he made regular entries from 1766 to 1824—most of his life. He recorded his observations of the local plant life from season to season, and drew up plans for Monticello's gardens before the house existed.

The Jeffersons moved to the Monticello property when they returned from their honeymoon and lived in a one-room brick building until the beautiful main house was habitable. Work continued on Jefferson's dream house until 1823, nearly the rest of his life.

Sadly, the couple lost several babies, and only two of their children, Martha "Patsy" and Maria "Polly," would live to adulthood. Mrs. Jefferson died in 1782, several months after giving birth to her last child, who died two years later. The loss of his wife was devastating to Jefferson. After her funeral, he stayed in his room for three weeks and, for some time after, he kept to himself—riding his horse around the countryside.

As a single father raising two daughters, Thomas Jefferson was devoted, attentive, and sometimes pushy. Not unlike Miss Amelia Hornsby, he was always teaching, always striving, always asking questions, and he was nothing if not opinionated. He was also an anxious father, and sometimes turned to John Adams's wife, Abigail, for advice on raising young girls.

Jefferson and his daughter Patsy were especially close, and some of their extensive correspondence survives. Patsy was said to resemble her father, being tall, pale, and angular, with red hair. While Jefferson served as the United States minister to France, Patsy lived in Paris, where she was enrolled in an exclusive convent school.

The letters Jefferson wrote to her while she was in school were often full of advice. He hoped, he once wrote, that "the moment you rise from your bed, your first work will be to dress yourself in such style, as that you may be seen by any gentlemen without his being able to discover a pin amiss, or any other circumstance of neatness wanting."

Jefferson was always inquiring about the details of his daughters' lives. "I am anxious to know what books you read, what tunes you play, and to receive specimens of your drawing," he wrote to Patsy. And his love for them was undeniable. Jefferson wrote to Patsy while they were separated: "The conviction that you would be more improved in the situation I have placed you than if still with me, has solaced me on my parting with you, which my love for you has rendered a difficult thing."

Maria Jefferson, known to her family as Polly, is said to have resembled her mother. After her father and Patsy had gone to France, Polly traveled to London. There, she was cared for by Abigail Adams, whose husband was then the U.S. minister to England. Later, she traveled to Paris, where she was enrolled in the same boarding school as her sister, Patsy.

Jefferson saw to it that his daughters received a better education than did most girls of that era. More importantly, he equipped them to continue learning throughout their lives, teaching them the importance of observation, reading, and curiosity about people and ideas.

Eighteen hundred and four was a good year for Jefferson's presidency, but a very sad year for the Jefferson family. Polly Jefferson Eppes died at the age of twenty-five from complications related to the birth of her second child.

After leaving the White House, Jefferson spent the last seventeen years of his life at Monticello surrounded by his grandchildren. He directed their education, gave them the books and gifts he thought suited their individual characters, and encouraged their interests. And he was a doting grandfather. Thomas Jefferson's grandchildren had the run of Monticello, sliding across the polished floors in their stocking feet!

Jefferson was a man whose wide range of interests and skills led him to innovate in many areas. In designing Monticello, he built in such unique features as an alcove bed—he could get out of bed on the right side and be in his office; his bedroom was on the left side of the bed. At the foot of the bed was a closet, or alcove, that held a special clothes horse with forty-eight projecting rods. His clothes hung here, and he could reach for them, or turn the clothes horse around by using a special stick. A two-faced clock at Monticello was visible from both the inside and the outside of the house.

Intrigued by new devices, he kept a polygraph, or copying machine, that made duplicate copies of his letters as he wrote them. Jefferson is also credited by most people as the inventor of the swivel chair, having designed for himself a chair that turned on its base so that he could reach different work areas with ease. He also designed a tilting table that could be adjusted for convenience depending on whether he was writing or sketching, standing or sitting. On his desk, he kept a swiveling bookstand so that he could have up to four different books open at one time, turning the stand like a lazy Susan in order to see the book he needed.

As a farmer, he learned the art of cultivating some "exotic" plants not commonly grown in this country, including special wine grapes, and garlic, which he attempted to grow at Monticello. He was given an award by a French agricultural society for designing a plow that turned up soil more efficiently.

An imaginative and inventive man, Thomas Jefferson was more than an accomplished politician, diplomat, and devoted father. His legacy has been a lasting one in both large and small ways. Among his many contributions, Jefferson was founder of the University of Virginia, which opened in 1825. Also, it was the sale of his personal library to Congress in 1815 that formed the core of our national library, now known as the Library of Congress. Early in his career, he established the use of the decimal system in the new United States. As an architect, he played a part in the building of the Capitol in Washington, D.C.

If you are interested in learning more about Thomas Jefferson's life and presidency, or about the details of the Lewis and Clark expedition, please visit this book's homepage at our interactive Web site at winslowpress.com.

Books written for kids

Blumberg, Rhoda, ed. *What's the Deal? Jefferson, Napoleon, and the Louisiana Purchase*. Washington, D.C.: National Geographic Society, 1998. This entertaining history of the Louisiana Territory will be especially interesting to anyone who's curious about the Lewis and Clark expedition (and about Thomas Jefferson's fascination with the American West).

Bohner, Charles. *Bold Journey: West with Lewis and Clark*. Boston: Houghton Mifflin Co., 1990. This adventure story is told from the point of view of Private Hugh McNeal as he accompanied Lewis and Clark on their expedition.

Clark, William. *Off the Map: The Journals of Lewis and Clark*. Connie Roop and Peter Roop, eds. Illustrated by Tim Tanner. New York: Walker & Co., 1998. This book is comprised of excerpts from the journals of Meriwether Lewis and William Clark, detailing their experiences during their expedition.

Fisher, Leonard Everett. *Monticello*. New York: Holiday House, 1988. This is a look at Thomas Jefferson's home, from his early designs of the house to his later life there.

Monsell, Helen Albee. *Tom Jefferson: Third President of the United States (Childhood of Famous Americans)*. Illustrated by Kenneth Wagner. New York: Aladdin Paperbacks, 1989. This is the story of Thomas Jefferson's early life.

O'Dell, Scott. *Streams to the River, River to the Sea*. Boston: Houghton Mifflin Co., 1997. This moving novel by the award-winning author of *Island of the Blue Dolphins* tells the story of Sacagawea and her travels with Lewis and Clark.

Smith, Roland. *The Captain's Dog: My Journey With the Lewis and Clark Tribe*. Orlando: Gulliver Books, 1999. Seaman, Captain Meriwether Lewis's dog, shares his perspective on the expedition. Includes excerpts from Lewis's diary.

St. George, Judith. *Sacagawea*. New York: Philomel Books, 1997. This fascinating, adventure-filled biography of Sacagawea, focuses on her journey with Lewis and Clark.

Books that kids and adults can enjoy

Ambrose, Stephen E. *Undaunted Courage: Meriwether Lewis, Thomas Jefferson, and the Opening of the American West*. New York: Simon & Schuster, 1997.

Bakeless, John. *Lewis and Clark: Partners in Discovery*. Mineola, NY: Dover Publications, 1996 (reprint of William Morrow & Co. 1946 title).

Baron, Robert C. and Henry Steele Commager, eds. *The Garden and Farm Books of Thomas Jefferson*. Golden, CO: Fulcrum Pubs., 1988. This includes selections from Jefferson's correspondence with John Adams, James Madison, and others about farming. His garden and farm journals are reproduced, as are a number of his drawings, plans, and sketches.

Betts, Edwin M. and James A. Bear, Jr., eds. *The Family Letters of Thomas Jefferson*. Charlottesville: University of Virginia Press, 1986.

Cunningham, Noble E., Jr. *The Pursuit of Reason: The Life of Thomas Jefferson*. New York: Ballantine Books, 1988. This biography of the third president is written for adult readers.

Duncan, Dayton. *Lewis & Clark: The Journey of the Corps of Discovery*. Ken Burns, contributor. New York: Knopf, 1997. This book is a companion volume to Ken Burns's documentary, and provides a good sense of the people and places involved in the Lewis and Clark expedition, including photographs of key locations, sketches from the journals, paintings, and many other illustrations.

McDonald, Forrest. *The Presidency of Thomas Jefferson*. Wichita: The University Press of Kansas, 1976. This study of Jefferson's presidency and politics is written for adult readers.

McLaughlin, Jack. *Jefferson and Monticello: The Biography of a Builder*. New York: Henry Holt, 1990. This is the story of Thomas Jefferson traced through his involvement in the design and building of his home.

Moeller, Bill and Jan Moeller. *Lewis and Clark: A Photographic Journey*. Missoula, MT: Mountain Press Publishing Company, 1999. These photographers traced the journey of Lewis and Clark, taking pictures of many sites associated with the expedition.

Randolph, Sarah N. *The Domestic Life of Thomas Jefferson, Compiled from Family Letters and Reminiscences*. Charlottesville: The Thomas Jefferson Memorial Foundation, 1994 (reprint of 1871 edition published by Harper, New York).

Schmidt, Thomas and Jeremy Schmidt. *Saga of Lewis and Clark: Into the Unknown West*. New York: Dorling Kindersley, 1999. Two brothers, one a naturalist/explorer and one a historian/writer, explore the story of Lewis and Clark. This book includes period illustrations, drawings from the journals, photographs, and more.

Tierney, Tom. *Thomas Jefferson and His Family: Paper Dolls in Full Color*. Mineola, NY: Dover Publications, 1992.

The text of Jefferson's *Autobiography* can be found on-line at http://www.bibliomania.com/NonFiction/Jefferson/Autobiography/chap00.html.

Here is a reproduction of an actual letter from Thomas Jefferson to Nicholas Van Zandt, written in 1807.

Amelia Hornsby's letters might have looked something like this:

Philadelphia, June 10, 1803

To Mr. Thomas Jefferson, President
Washington City

Dear Sir,

I most humbly beg your pardon.
I am not yet in society, having passed
through a mere twelve years on this
earth. This is why I reside with
Dr. Rush while waiting for my father
to establish a home for me on the
frontier at Pittsburgh. My mother was
taken in the yellow fever epidemic in
1798, as were my sisters and brothers.
I alone survive with my father.

From poor
Amelia Hornsby, Half-orphan

About the U.S. Postal Service, 1804

When Thomas Jefferson and Amelia Hornsby conducted their fictitious correspondence in the early years of the nineteenth century, they were using a postal system established a quarter-century earlier by Benjamin Franklin.

In 1775, Franklin was appointed to be this country's first postmaster general, a job he held for just over a year. An effective system for delivering mail was essential to an independent government, and Franklin's job was to develop that system. The postal service we use today descends directly from the one planned by Benjamin Franklin.

In 1781, Congress was given the responsibility for establishing and regulating post offices throughout the new country.

In 1800, the postal headquarters was moved to Washington, D.C. At this time, much of the nation's mail was delivered by carriers traveling on foot and by horseback along the country's postal roads.

The Post Office Department began to purchase stagecoaches, which could carry larger amounts of mail along these roads. It is likely that the Jefferson-Hornsby correspondence would have been carried by stagecoach on the well-traveled roads between Washington and Philadelphia.

More information on the history of the United Sates Postal Service can be found online at http://www.usps.gov/history.

Interactive Web Footnotes

Here is an alphabetical list of the interactive footnotes found at the bottom of the pages in this book. We hope that this list will prove to be an easy reference for locating the subjects you are interested in at this book's own Web site at **winslowpress.com**.

Aaron Burr
American Philosophical Society
Animals discovered by Lewis and Clark
Archaeology in the 19th century
Benjamin Rush, Dr.
Charles Willson Peale
Corps of Discovery
Declaration of Independence
Duel between Aaron Burr and Alexander Hamilton
Early American almanacs
Education in the 19th century
Entertainment in the 1880s
Expressions used in the 1880s
Fire-fighting in the 19th century
First Americans and the pioneers
Free Africa Society
Fur trade
Inventions of the early 1880s
Jefferson's family
Jefferson's weather journals
Lewis and Clark expedition
Louisiana Purchase
Meriwether Lewis

Monticello

19th century newspapers

Oliver Evans and the *Orukter Amphibolis*

Philadelphia

Philadelphia's waterworks

Pittsburgh

Relations between England and the United States

Repository for Natural Curiosities

Robert Fulton

Role of women in the 1880s

Sacagawea

Washington City

William Clark

York

Index

(Colored numbers represent photographs)

G

garden book, 28, 98
Great Britain, 78, 81, 82, 83, 84, 91, 92, 94, 97

H

Hamilton, Alexander, 48, 49, 66
Hemmings, Sally, 92
Hidasta Indians, see Indians
Hudson River, see river

I

Independence Hall, 13, 17, 66
Indians, 23, 24, 30, 32, 60, 61, 76, 95; Ahwahharway, 58;
Arikara, 58; Hidasta, 56, 58, 63, 64; Mandan, 58, 75, 76;
Minittarra, 58; Omaha, 50; Osage, 48, 76; Shoshoni, 58, 63, 77
inventions, general, 29; Jefferson's, 46, 63, 100, 101

J

Jean Baptiste, 58, 64
Jefferson family, 44, 89, 90, 97, 98, 99, 100, 101
Jefferson, Jane Randolph, 89
Jefferson, Maria "Polly," 44, 99, 100
Jefferson, Martha "Patsy," 46, 47, 98, 99
Jefferson, Peter, 89, 90
Jefferson, Thomas, 11, 45, 82, 84, 87
Jones, Reverend Absolom, 60

K

keelboat, 30, 34

L

M

N

O

Ohio River, see rivers
Omaha Indians, see Indians
Orukter Amphibolis, 62, 63
Osage Indians, see Indians

P

Peale, Charles Willson, 32, 33, 35, 46, 58, 63, 66, 66, 77
Peale Museum, 70, 71
Philadelphia, 9, 13, 13, 16, 17, 23, 27, 29, 36, 41, 47, 48, 50, 51,
54, 55, 56, 58, 60, 62, 66, 69, 70, 71, 84
Philadelphia Repository, 54
Philosophical Hall, 32
Pike, Lieutenant Zebulon, 65, 65
Pittsburgh, 20, 24, 30, 34, 48, 50, 52, 53, 58, 69, 70, 74, 84
plants, 18, 23, 30, 86
Port Folio, 43, 54
Postal Service, 108, 109

R

rivers, Columbia River, 72, 76; Delaware River, 29, 62, 70;
Hudson River, 70; Marias River, 77; Mississippi River, 22, 24, 25,
38, 56, 65, 94; Missouri River, 22, 23, 24, 25, 38, 56, 64, 72, 77,
81, 95, 96; Ohio River, 34; Schuylkill River, 24, 54, 56, 62; Seine
River, 33; Yellowstone River, 77
Rocky Mountains, 58, 77, 94
Rush, Dr. Benjamin, 15, 16, 18, 19, 19, 21, 22, 23, 38, 44, 47, 50,
51, 58, 70
Rush, Mrs. Benjamin, 19, 22, 29, 50

S

Sacagawea, 58, 60, 61, 62, 63, 64, 66, 75, 77, 84

Winslow Press wishes to acknowledge the following sources
for the photographs and illustrations in this book:

All of the illustrative material is courtesy of the Library of Congress,
except for the fire water buckets on pages 42 and 43,
which are courtesy of New York City Fire Museum,
and the maps on pages 22, 23, 25, and 35,
which are courtesy of the David Rumsey Historical Map Collection.

Cover illustration © 2000 by Mark Summers

DEAR MR. PRESIDENT and the DEAR MR. PRESIDENT logo
are registered trademarks of Winslow Press.

Thanks to R. Sean Wilentz, Dayton-Stockton Professor of History, and Director,
Program in American Studies, Princeton University, for evaluating the manuscript.

Armstrong, Jennifer, 1961–
Thomas Jefferson : letters from a Philadelphia bookworm / written by Jennifer Armstrong. —1st ed.
p. cm. — (Dear Mr. President)
Includes bibliographical references and index.
Summary: An educated, inquisitive young girl in Philadelphia corresponds with President Thomas
Jefferson about current events, including the Lewis and Clark expedition, new inventions,
and life at Monticello.
ISBN: 1-890817-30-9
1. Jefferson, Thomas, 1743–1826—Juvenile fiction. [1. Jefferson, Thomas, 1743–1826—Fiction. 2.
Presidents—Fiction. 3. United States—History—1801–1809—Fiction. 4. Letters—Fiction.] I. Title.

PZ7.A73367 T1 2000
[Fic]—dc21
00-020528

Creative Director: Bretton Clark
Designer: Victoria Stehl
Editor: Margery Cuyler

Printed in the United States of America
First Edition
10 9 8 7 6 5 4 3 2 1

**DISCOVER WORLDWIDE LINKS, GAMES, ACTIVITIES, AND MORE
AT OUR INTERACTIVE WEB SITE:**

WINSLOWPRESS.COM.

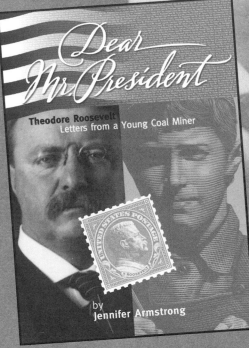